Better Than You Think

By Eduardo Díaz
Illustrated by Pat Paris

Copyright © 2000 Metropolitan Teaching and Learning Company.
Published by Metropolitan Teaching and Learning Company.
Printed in the United States of America.
All rights reserved. No part of this work may be reproduced, transmitted, or utilized in any form or by any means, electronic, mechanical, or otherwise, including photocopying and recording, or by any storage and retrieval system, without prior written permission from
Metropolitan Teaching and Learning Company, 33 Irving Place, New York, NY 10003.

ISBN 1-58120-041-2

3 4 5 6 7 8 9 CL 03 02 01

"I don't think you stink," said Lin. "You're better than you think. You never drop the ball. You throw well. You could get kids out."

"Say you will stay, Dan," said Jed.

"You're right, I will stay for a little bit," said Dan. "I will sit in the stands and yell. And I will have some pink lemonade. Where is it?"

"The pink lemonade is over there," said Lin. "And there is Mr. Grant. He runs our team."

"Mr. Grant," said Lin. "This is our friend Dan. He came to see us play."

"Good," said Mr. Grant. "We have time before the other kids get here. I will pitch and you two can hit. You can play, too, Dan."

"Thank you," said Dan. "But I don't play very well. I never get a hit. I never get a run. I stink at this game."

"Don't say that. You may be better than you think," said Mr. Grant. "Come and play with us."

"Look at the ball when I throw," said Mr. Grant. "Think about where the ball is going."

"I think I can do that," said Dan.

"When you get the ball, throw it here," said Jed. "I will throw it to Lin."

"You didn't drop the ball, Dan," said Lin. "You're very good. Would you like to pitch?"

"Do you think I could?" asked Dan.

"Sure you can," said Jed. "You have what it takes."

"Our friend Dan can pitch," said Jed. "He can throw the ball better than I can."

"Will you pitch, Dan?" asked Mr. Grant.

"I will pitch," said Dan. "But I didn't come to play. Don't get mad if we don't win!"

"I didn't think you would play, Dan," said Lin. "I'm glad you said you would."

"That is what friends are for," said Dan. "But I wish I could play better. What if I can't pitch?"

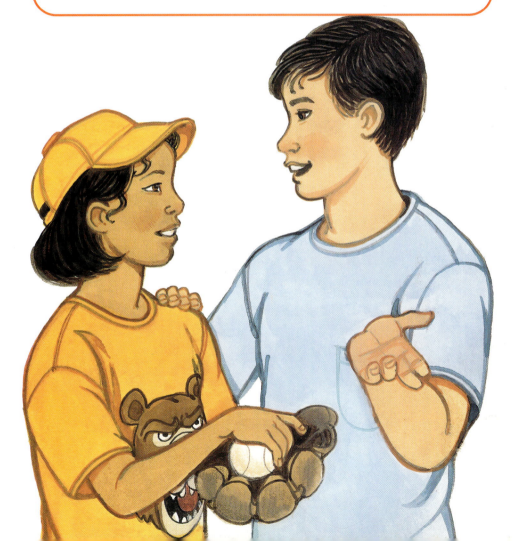

"You can do it, Dan," said Lin. "Put it right over home plate!"

"That was a good throw!" yelled Jed. "Look where it went. It went right over home plate. No one can say you don't pitch well, Dan!"

"A home run!" yelled Dan. "I can't pitch!"

"The ball went right over home plate again," said Mr. Grant. "All the kids can hit a ball like that. Throw a low ball. Drop your hand a little bit. Let the ball go when your hand is low."

"I did throw a low pitch that time," said Dan. "But that kid hit it."

"But the hit was right to me at first," said Jed. "I got it and the kid was out!"

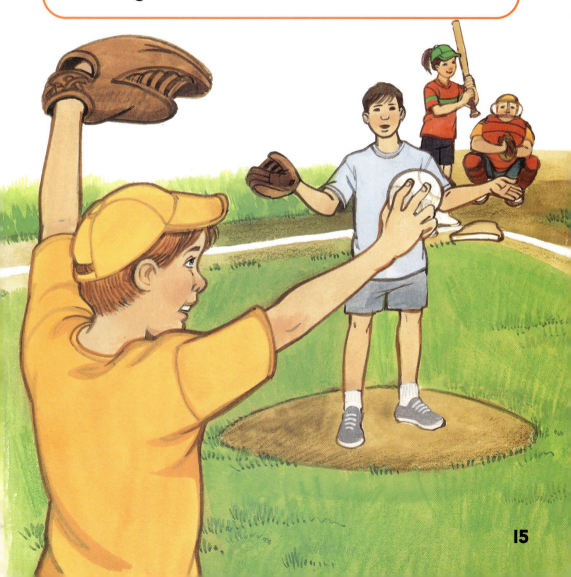

"We didn't win, kids," said Mr. Grant. "But thanks to you, we got your friend to pitch. You can pitch for me any day, Dan."

"Thanks, Mr. Grant," said Dan. "I had a lot of fun. And lots of pink lemonade to drink."